Penelope Nuthatch

and the Big Surprise

David Gavril

Harry N. Abrams, Inc., Publishers

For my sister, Elizabeth, and my grandfather, Cornelius Van Leeuwen

Artist's Note
The artwork in this book was created with pencil, ink,
and watercolor paints on Arches paper.

Designed by Celina Carvalho
Production Manager: Jonathan Lopes

Library of Congress Cataloging-in-Publication Data:
Gavril, David.
Penelope Nuthatch / written and illustrated by David Gavril.
p. cm.
Summary: Penelope Nuthatch excitedly prepares for a surprise outing with her friend by having her
feathers fluffed, but then she learns that they are going to a water park.
ISBN 0-8109-5762-0
[1. Amusement parks—Fiction. 2. Surprise—Fiction. 3. Birds—Fiction.] I. Title.

PZ7.G2358Pen 2006
[E]—dc22
2005015258

Printed and bound in China
10 9 8 7 6 5 4 3 2 1

Harry N. Abrams, Inc.
115 West 18th Street
New York, NY 10011
www.abramsbooks.com

Abrams is a subsidiary of
LA MARTINIÈRE
GROUPE

One morning, Penelope Nuthatch received an invitation from her
good friend Luther. It said, "Dear Penelope, Mr. Luther Crow requests
your presence for an unforgettable surprise. I will pick you up today at
one o'clock."

Penelope was so excited. She had never been anywhere "unforgettable" before, at least not that she could recall. What could Luther's surprise be?

With her feathers still fluttering, she sat down to read the morning newspaper. An interesting item caught her eye.

Penelope called Luther. "I got your invitation," she said. She waited for him to say where they were going.

But all Luther said was, "It's going to be wonderful!"

Wonderful, she thought after she hung up the phone. *Unforgettable* . . . Penelope looked at her paper. Why, it had to be *Swan Lake*!

"Yippee!" she chirped, "I've been dying to see *Swan Lake*. I'd better go get my feathers fluffed."

Penelope sang as she pedaled over to see Madame Twigg at the beauty parlor.

"First ze bubbles," said Madame Twigg. "Heads up for ze pins!" Then, after a whoosh of her blow dryer, she combed Penelope's plume.

"Ooo-la-la, you look *fantastique*," cried Madame Twigg. "Enjoy your fancy feathers!"

Back at her nest, Penelope looked for something special to wear.

Finally, she settled on her lavender tutu. "Perfect!" she exclaimed.

Penelope heard Luther's car and ran outside.
"Howdy, Penelope!" said Luther.
"You're early," said Penelope.
"Early bird gets the worm," Luther replied.

"Are you ready?"

"Ready?" said Penelope. "I can hardly wait!" And she did a little twirl.

"You're really going to be surprised," said Luther. "Cover your eyes, please."

"Are we there yet?" asked Penelope every time Luther stopped at a traffic light. "Are we there yet?" she whispered whenever they went slowly up a hill.

But Luther kept driving. When they finally rolled to a halt, Penelope opened her eyes.

They were in front of a huge sign. It said, "Welcome to Wet and Wild Water World!"

"Yippee," yelled Luther, tossing his hat. "Isn't this a terrific surprise?"

Penelope was so disappointed her feathers sagged.
"Let's try the bumper boats first!" said Luther.
"I think you'd better go without me," said Penelope.

As Luther ricocheted across the pond, Penelope fanned herself.
My plume is melting, she thought. *I wish I could find some shade.*

"Hop in and ride the whale waves," yelled Luther. "It's a blast!"

"I'd rather not," said Penelope. The hot sun was making her dizzy and her cotton candy was sticking to her feathers.

"You look hot," said Luther. "Let's cool down on the Octopus Dunker!"
"No, thank you," said Penelope.
"In that case," said Luther, "I'll buy you an ice cream cone."

"One strawberry birdseed crunch coming right up!"
But just as Luther bought the cone, a passing elephant crashed into him.

The ice cream went flying and landed *plop*! on Penelope's head. Luther looked at Penelope's sticky feathers and sour face. "I'm sorry you're not having any fun," he said. "I guess this wasn't a wonderful surprise. Maybe we should go home."

On their way out, they passed by Penguin Point.

A penguin was making an announcement.

"CANNONBALL!"

Penelope was thoroughly drenched.

She shook out her feathers. She was no longer sticky. In fact, she was deliciously cool.

Suddenly, she knew what she wanted to do.

"Would you join me for a tumble on the Otter Slide?" Penelope asked.
"Really?" said Luther.
"Race you to the ladder!"

"Hold onto your feathers!" yelled Luther.
SPLASH!

Penelope and Luther spent the rest of the day splashing, sliding, and, of course, cannonballing, until Luther got water in his beak and asked to be taken home.

And the next week Penelope had a surprise for Luther.